Family Folklore

North American Folklore

Children's Folklore
Christmas and Santa Claus Folklore
Contemporary Folklore
Ethnic Folklore
Family Folklore
Firefighters' Folklore
Folk Arts and Crafts
Folk Customs
Folk Dance
Folk Fashion
Folk Festivals
Folk Games
Folk Medicine
Folk Music
Folk Proverbs and Riddles
Folk Religion
Folk Songs
Folk Speech
Folk Tales and Legends
Food Folklore
Regional Folklore

North American Folklore

Family Folklore

BY SHIRLEY BRINKERHOFF
AND ELLYN SANNA

Mason Crest Publishers

Mason Crest Publishers Inc.
370 Reed Road
Broomall, Pennsylvania 19008
(866) MCP-BOOK (toll free)
www.masoncrest.com

First printing
1 2 3 4 5 6 7 8 9 10
Library of Congress Cataloging-in-Publication Data on file at the Library of Congress.
ISBN 1-59084-333-9
      1-59084-328-2 (series)

Design by Lori Holland.
Composition by Bytheway Publishing Services, Binghamton, New York.
Cover design by Joe Gilmore.
Printed and bound in the Hashemite Kingdom of Jordan.

Picture credits:
Corbis: pp. 83, 89, 90
Corel: pp. 53, 57
Eclectic Collections: pp. 6, 8, 20, 32, 48, 60, 84, 96, 99
PhotoAlto: pp. 85, 92
PhotoDisc: pp. 11, 12, 14, 15, 16, 22, 26, 27, 30, 34, 36, 38, 39, 40, 42, 43, 44, 50, 52,
          55, 56, 62, 64, 66, 68, 69, 70, 72, 74, 76, 78, 79, 81, 86, 87, 94, 100
Cover: "After Dinner Homework" by Herman Geisen © 1947 SEPS: Licensed by Curtis
          Publishing, Indianapolis, IN. www.curtispublishing.com

Contents

Folklore grows from long-ago
seeds. Just as an acorn sends
down roots even as it shoots up
leaves across the sky, folklore is
rooted deeply in the past and
yet still lives and grows today.
It spreads through our modern
world with branches as wide
and sturdy as any oak's;
it grounds us in yesterday even
as it helps us make sense of
both the present and the future.

INTRODUCTION

by Dr. Alan Jabbour

W HAT DO A TALE, a joke, a fiddle tune, a quilt, a jig, a game of jacks, a saint's day procession, a snake fence, and a Halloween costume have in common? Not much, at first glance, but all these forms of human creativity are part of a zone of our cultural life and experience that we sometimes call "folklore."

The word "folklore" means the cultural traditions that are learned and passed along by ordinary people as part of the fabric of their lives and culture. Folklore may be passed along in verbal form, like the urban legend that we hear about from friends who assure us that it really happened to a friend of their cousin. Or it may be tunes or dance steps we pick up on the block, or ways of shaping things to use or admire out of materials readily available to us, like that quilt our aunt made. Often we acquire folklore without even fully realizing where or how we learned it.

Though we might imagine that the word "folklore" refers to cultural traditions from far away or long ago, we actually use and enjoy folklore as part of our own daily lives. It is often ordinary, yet we often remember and prize it because it seems somehow very special. Folklore is culture we share with others in our communities, and we build our identities through the sharing. Our first shared identity is family identity, and family folklore such as shared meals or prayers or songs helps us develop a sense of belonging. But as we grow older we learn to belong to other groups as well. Our identities may be ethnic, religious, occupational, or regional—or all of these, since no one has only one cultural identity. But in every case, the identity is anchored and strengthened by a variety of cultural traditions in which we participate and share with our neighbors. We feel the threads of connection with people we know, but the threads extend far beyond our own immediate communities. In a real sense, they connect us in one way or another to the world.

Folklore possesses features by which we distinguish ourselves from each other. A certain dance step may be African American, or a certain story urban, or a certain hymn Protestant, or a certain food preparation Cajun. Folklore can distinguish us, but at the same time it is one of the best ways we introduce ourselves to each other. We learn about new ethnic groups on the North American landscape by sampling their cuisine, and we enthusiastically adopt musical ideas from other communities. Stories, songs, and visual designs move from group to group, enriching all people in the process. Folklore thus is both a sign of identity, experienced as a special marker of our special groups, and at the same time a cultural coin that is well spent by sharing with others beyond our group boundaries.

Folklore is usually learned informally. Somebody, somewhere, taught us that jump rope rhyme we know, but we may have trouble remembering just where we got it, and it probably wasn't in a book that was assigned as homework. Our world has a domain of formal knowledge, but folklore is a domain of knowledge and culture that is learned by sharing and imitation rather than formal instruction. We can study it formally—that's what we are doing now!—but its natural arena is in the informal, person-to-person fabric of our lives.

Not all culture is folklore. Classical music, art sculpture, or great novels are forms of high art that may contain folklore but are not themselves folklore. Popular music or art may be built on folklore themes and traditions, but it addresses a much wider and more diverse audience than folk music or folk art. But even in the world of popular and mass culture, folklore keeps popping up around the margins. E-mail is not folklore—but an e-mail smile is. And college football is not folklore—but the wave we do at the stadium is.

This series of volumes explores the many faces of folklore throughout the North American continent. By illuminating the many aspects of folklore in our lives, we hope to help readers of the series to appreciate more fully the richness of the cultural fabric they either possess already or can easily encounter as they interact with their North American neighbors.

Families have always given their members a sense of belonging.

ONE

The Meaning
of Family
A Sense of Belonging

The story of the Ugly Duckling demonstrates the importance of feeling as though we are accepted and loved by others like ourselves.

How Surprised

OW SURPRISED the mother duck was when the biggest egg in her nest finally hatched. But the creature that emerged from the broken shell looked nothing like the rest of her brood.

"Look how big he is!" the mother said to her ducklings. "Much bigger than any of you."

"Ugly, too," one of the ducklings agreed. "Our feathers are yellow, but his are a dull gray."

"He doesn't talk like us, either," quacked another duckling.

The ugly duckling was so mistreated by the others that he ran away. He found a group of wild ducks living on a pond nearby, but when he tried to join them, they said the same things about him.

"You don't look like us!"

"You don't talk like us!"

"Go away!"

They flapped their wings at him and quacked loudly, scaring the ugly little duckling.

He came to a barnyard where a flock of chickens pecked at kernels of corn. "May I eat corn with you?" he asked shyly.

The hen cocked her head and looked him over. "Hmmm, you're a strange looking one. And you talk funny, too."

The ugly duckling knew what was coming, and he left the barnyard before the hen could drive him away.

For a short time, the poor little duckling took shelter in the home of an old lady with a cat. He tried to make friends with the cat. He even tried to act like the cat, since the lady seemed so fond of it. But within just a day or two, the duckling's longing to be in the water overwhelmed him.

"The water?" purred the cat. "You want to go into the *water*?" He arched his back and gave a loud meow. "You're a strange, strange creature."

At last, tired and sad and longing to find a family of his own, the ugly duckling came to a pond where he saw the most beautiful birds he could imagine. He watched them for an entire day, hiding in the bushes so they wouldn't drive him away. Sometimes the beautiful big birds swam gracefully, their long slender necks reflected in the calm water beneath them. The ugly duckling stretched his neck as far as he could, and felt his own legs ache to swim with them. Sometimes the magnifi- cent birds flew, their powerful white wings sweeping the air and lifting them high above the trees. The ugly duckling flapped his own wings and, though he tried to be silent, he could not help making one little cry—his own cry that all the other animals had found so strange.

Immediately, the huge birds heard him and answered with cries that sounded just like his. They flew to where he was hiding and landed on the water in front of his bushes. "Come and swim with us!" they said, welcoming him.

The ugly duckling was afraid to join them at first. "I can't. I'm just an ugly duckling," he said.

The big birds said, "No, you are one of us!"

The duckling couldn't believe it, but when they finally coaxed him into the water, he caught sight of his own reflection. He was no longer gray. His feathers were white now, like theirs. His neck had grown as long and as graceful as theirs. He spread his wings with delight and saw that they looked as powerful as the wings of these beautiful birds.

"You are one of us," cried the swans, and he swam away with them, overjoyed to find his real family at last.

FINDING a family of one's own is a major theme in literature, especially children's literature. Humans come into the world with a longing to belong to one group of people above all others, to be loved and accepted and cherished unconditionally, as the ugly duckling finally was.

How do families satisfy that innate desire to belong? Perhaps the basic component is sharing. Families share a history, a present, and hopes for the future.

"Happy families are all alike," Leo Tolstoy wrote in *Anna Karenina*. While everyone may not agree with the Russian novelist, it is obvious to folklorists that families share many similar traditions and customs—conducting ceremonies to mark special days or milestones in family members' lives; celebrating holidays in unique ways; telling jokes and using phrases that no one but family members understand. All of these distinguishing characteristics and many, many more sketch out the identity of a family. They clearly mark one group of people

A family should be a place where ideas and creativity can flourish.

Even family pets have their place in family folklore.

as a unit, as being inside certain boundaries, and just as clearly show that others are outside.

One modern commentator on the breakup of the family said, "Every divorce is the death of a small civilization," and "a small civilization" is one good way to define a family, because a family's customs and traditions—its folklore— marks it as a unique entity, a small civilization of its own.

Defining "family" has become a topic of intense debate in the 21st century, with sometimes heated disagreement over the components of a family. Rather than define family by its composition, however, author Edith Schaeffer defines it by function. According to her book, *What Is a Family*, a family is

- a *mobile* unit of connected human beings who interact in constantly changing patterns, "affected by each other, inspired by each other, helped by each other, with roots in the past and stretching out into the future."
- the birthplace of creativity, where an atmosphere of trust brings forth a sharing of ideas and an attempt to make something new. "Creativity needs an audience, some appreciation, the response of another human being, as well as . . . freedom. . . ."

- a formation center for human relationships, "the place where the deep understanding that people are significant, important, worthwhile, with a purpose in life, should be learned at an early age."
- a shelter in the time of storm, where "the knowledge of what is necessary for basic care . . . and thoughtfulness . . . should be absorbed through years of living . . . pleasant moments in the middle of misery, assurance of love in the midst of fear. . . ."
- an educational context, where the responsibility is met to educate both the next generation and the one that comes after, training children "intellectually, spiritually, culturally, emotionally—in things of creativity, in understanding the whole of history, in relationships with other people. . . ."
- a museum of memories, where overlapping recollections can be shared, integrated, and treasured.

Family stability . . . is an achievement in group living. In this process of living together, there are certain techniques which make for success. . . . Family life is a social process. It has a definite cultural content. Its relationships are intimate, repetitious, and continue over long periods of time. Many patterns of behavior come to be prescribed, both for the individual and for family functioning as a whole.

—James H. S. Bossard and Eleanor S. Boll, *Ritual in Family Living*

FAMILIES MATTER

People need to experience the beauty of being part of a mobile art form, and people who have never known such beauty exists need to see it taking place. If human relationships are to be beautiful on a wider form, . . . the individual families making up society have to be really worked on by someone who understands that artists have to *work* to produce their art.

—*Edith Schaeffer*

The family is where we form our earliest and often most significant relationships.

Not all families are traditional—but the best ones are built on love.

Family folklore is the means by which families accomplish many of these tasks. A shared collection of stories, traditions, foods, songs, and jokes gives families a sense of ongoing unity. These unique customs glue each family together.

The word "custom" is defined by Jan Harold Brunvand as a traditional practice, "a mode of individual behavior or a habit of social life . . . that is transmitted by word of mouth or imitation, then ingrained by social pressure, common usage, and parental or other authority." The author goes on to explain that the ways in which we pass on folklore is in itself customary. When a grandfather tells a family story, or an aunt sings a ballad passed down from forebears, they are choosing a means to transmit the store of family folklore, and the means chosen becomes a family custom itself.

Most American folk customs are associated with special events. Birth, marriage, and death are among the more important "rites of passage," and special customs have grown up around these events to make them stand out in some way or ways from everyday existence.

Family folklore includes not only customs

The study of traditional customs is known as *ethnography*. When ethnographers study the *folklife* of different groups, stories, songs, foods, celebrations, and jokes are just some of the material they study.

> Some family traditions can be as simple as sitting down together for the evening meal or as elaborate as dressing in special clothes to celebrate a holiday. Whatever way your family chooses to perform traditions, most family experts agree that even the little things that you enjoy over and over again within your family form a lasting impression on you and other family members. How would you describe your family's traditions for the following events?
>
> • visiting with relatives
> • family reunions
> • family fun (activities like biking, bowling, picnics, etc.)
> • mealtimes
> • birthdays

but stories and retellings and vocabulary. Authors Steven J. Zeitlin, Amy J. Kotkin, and Holly Cutting Baker point out in *A Celebration of American Family Folklore* that family folklore differs from family history in that family folklore is the "personalized and often creative distillations of experience, worked and re-worked over time. . . . a glorious moment carefully selected and elaborated through the years, tailored to the demands of the present."

Out of these selections from their common past, each family weaves a fabric that binds them together in many ways. Sometimes a simple custom, such as saying the little poem quoted in chapter two when walking down a sidewalk, is passed on to children by an older member of the family and helps link the gener-

Children learn to be the parents of the next generation even while they are still children.

ations together. If the child then chooses to pass the custom on to his or her own children, it will probably be introduced with, "My grandma [or grandpa or uncle or aunt, etc.] always said this to me when we went for a walk," providing a sense of continuity that links the generations.

Many families have a storyteller or mimic among their members, as described in chapter three, a person who transmits by word or imitation some characteristic of an older relative (Uncle Joe's interminable war stories, tee-totaling Grandma's habit of secreting a bottle of wine in the linen closet "for sore throats," that little "harrumph" noise Grandpa used to make when he was about to tell a joke), thus adding to the family's sense of unique identity.

Some families, as in chapter four, love each other through thick and thin. Other families feud until, as Mark Twain observed in *The Adventures of Huckleberry Finn*, "by and by everybody's killed off, and there ain't no more feud. But it's kind of slow, and takes a long time."

The concept people form of God is often shaped, for good or ill, by the behavior of their parents. The college professor described in chapter five felt intense fury whenever she heard the phrase "God the Father." Her family folklore was not positive when it came to fathers. Others who have had loving and nurturing parents grow up with an entirely different view of the divine.

Families also each have their own way of celebrating and mourning life's milestones. Chapter six deals with many of these, from lost teeth to graduation parties.

For most people, life is lived within the boundaries of some kind of family group. That group is one of the most powerful forces shaping the world's present generation of children, and through them, all the generations to come. The following chapters look at how families develop and maintain their individual family folklore—the stories they choose to pass along to the next generation, the hilarious expressions or the words mispronounced by a baby brother that become part of the private family vocabulary, the customs held sacred at every holiday or birthday—these are all part of the heritage that makes each family unique.

Family folklore serves to link the generations.

TWO

Linking the
Generations
The Family Legacy

Families pass along their traditions and beliefs, from grandparents to parents to children.

LIFE IS FULL of mysteries, especially in the minds of children. An editor of children's books frequently reminded her authors that, to a child, everything is new. Simon Bronner echoes this theme in *American Children's Folklore*. "Childhood is a time of questioning and wondering," he says. "Children call upon a host of beliefs and customs to make their way through an uncertain world." Many of these beliefs, continues Bronner, are planted in children's minds by parents or other relatives, who often want only to keep their children safe or help them grown into well-mannered adults.

Families have various ways of shaping the behavior of their younger members. Some of these may seem illogical; sometimes adults refuse to voice the real-life consequences of certain behaviors and devise lesser dire results instead; but the private language of warning and restriction functions within the unique environment of each family unit. "If you play with matches, you'll wet the bed," one family warns. Another family reminds the children regularly about the importance of not talking to strangers or getting into cars with them, then jokes about "Chester, the Molester," the fictitious character they've created to "lighten things up."

Some families have superstitions, sayings, or proverbs for every situation, even walking down the sidewalk. Common sayings include, "Step on a crack, break your mother's back," or "Step on the line, break your spine." Instead of voicing superstitions, one family goes for laughter and quotes the "Lines and Squares" poem by A. A. Milne (the author of the Winnie the Pooh stories):

Whenever I walk in a London street,
I'm ever so careful to watch my feet;

After hearing the poem for years, all three children can join in readily; it has become a tradition that has passed into the family folklore, and they will no doubt pass it on to their children as "something my mother always said to me when we went for a walk."

One family always addresses the grasshoppers they encounter in a most imperative way:

Grasshopper, grasshopper, grasshopper gray,
Grasshopper, grasshopper, get out of my way.

Even the youngest child in the family knows the story behind this little chant.

When Grandma was a five-year-old, she had to walk by herself several miles on dirt roads to the one-room schoolhouse. The large gray grasshoppers in the road ahead of her would freeze her in her tracks—until she learned to implore them to move with this two-line ditty. The grasshoppers would zip away on long, buzzing wings, and Grandma would continue on her way. Years later, she told the story to her daughter . . . who then passed it on to a third generation.

There was a time when the only means to pass on family memories was to tell a story, sing a song, or recite a poem.

Countless books, poems, and ballads have been written and composed with such an end in mind. With the passing of the years, however, people have found new ways to capture and pass on their memories.

First came grainy black and white

Sometimes the experiences of an earlier generation can offer strength to the present family. Author Daryl Cumber Dance, in *From My People*, includes this woman's family memory of a grandmother:

She had a little black hat and her hair just as white, white as snow, just as white as snow. And she been in slavery when it first start, when it first start. My grandma been a hundred and fifteen when she die. She say she had a time in slavery. . . . My grandma used to go with her dress tied round her waist and a big foot tub on her head, going down the road. . . . She say, "Children, all we that been in slavery got something to tell God when we get home. . . . You got to tell God all your troubles about this world below," she say. "I got a lot to tell him and plenty more."

daguerreotypes, then Kodak snapshots and self-developing Polaroid pictures. Now videos and digital images, sent in the blink of an eye through E-mail, all capture how a family member or members look in that brief moment. These images are tinged with sentiment and *nostalgia*, and the pictures themselves help shape future memories.

Taping, first audio alone, then audio and videotaping combined, now allows us to record both sight and sound. The quantity and variety of camcorders in use at elementary school programs and high school graduations attest to the immense popularity of taping. These records will pass into the *archives* of family folklore.

Even though taping has in some ways *superseded* photography, pictures remain an extremely important way of preserving family memories. As people have grown frustrated with inaccessible pictures stuffed into boxes or drawers, a new movement called "Creative Memories" has spread across America. People,

Family folklore is a bond that unites family members.

particularly women, attend seminars in which they are taught how to most effectively arrange their pictures into keepsake albums, with captions and decorations.

As the **baby boomers**' generation enters retirement age, enterprising publishers have brought out books that encourage the transmission of memories. While some older people are able to write out page after page of information on the customs, traditions, and memories of their families, others struggle to figure out how to begin. Books that get the process going and sometimes require no more than the filling in of a line or two in answer to a direct question are helpful in this area. These books provide a tangible place for storing the family's folklore.

Generations can be linked by both advice (and warning), and by communicating hope for the future. In both cases, it is usually the older generation that initiates the linking process.

LOVE STORIES: HOW OUR FAMILY CAME TO BE

What child doesn't enjoy hearing how his mother and father met and fell in love? Perhaps the perennial question "Where do babies come from?" is a quest for far more than the story of physical birth. All children long to know they were hoped for and born out of love shared by the two most important people in their world. And if the story includes a passionate romantic attraction that swept one or both of them off their feet, so much the better. In fact, according to the authors of *American Family Folklore,* it is likely that "selective remembering and after-the-fact interpretation often add an element of love at first sight. . . . Marriage bonds seem to be strengthened by the memory of a romantic, passionate courtship. . . . By the same token succeeding generations, exaggerating the romance still more, can look back at their progenitors as having been linked by mysterious and powerful passions. . . . In this sense, Americans think in reverse . . . replacing coincidence with destiny."

For instance, one family loves to tell the story of how Grandpa fell in love with Grandma. Grandma, it seems, had been a tough-minded, independent schoolteacher with no time in her

Our grandparents' love story may be a part of how we perceive our family.

FOOD AS A LINK TO THE PAST

Some families are linked by unique recipes or eating habits passed down through the generations. Some of these are everyday foods; others are for the special dishes prepared for holidays or celebrations.

One family, in which the parents had been raised during the **Depression**, still sometimes eat the foods that were available during that difficult period. These foods include mashed potato sandwiches for lunch, and cracker soup for breakfast. Mashed potato sandwiches are fairly self-explanatory, but for those who need help with cracker soup, here is the recipe:

Place saltine crackers in a cereal bowl. Pour hot coffee over the crackers, add a little whole milk and lots of sugar. (Enjoy *quickly*, before the crackers turn totally to mush.)

Children's author Stephanie Gordon Tessler recounts how she became the "keeper" of her grandma's famous kugel recipe (which she calls "Grandma Kepniss's To-Die-For Noodle Kugel), the one that made everyone in the family say, "Invite Grandma Kepniss, she can bring her fabulous noodle kugel!"

Tessler remembers that, by the time she became an adult, her mother, Sylvia Gordon, was the keeper of the recipe and everyone then said, "Invite Grandma Sylvia, she can bring her fabulous noodle kugel!"

Tessler now has the recipe and hopes her secret knowledge will "guarantee my invitations to all future family gatherings, so I will bring my fabulous noodle kugel!"

Adapted from *Writers In the Kitchen*, compiled by Tricia Gardella. Honesdale: Boyds Mills Press, 1998.

life for romance. Grandpa was five years younger, a dreamy farmer who had been late to settle down. Grandpa loved animals and dirt; Grandma loved books and cleanliness. They met accidentally at the post office; he knew from the first moment he saw her that he loved her—and from the moment she laid her eyes on him, she knew he was not for her.

But at a church supper two months later, they ended up sitting next to each other, and reluctantly, for courtesy sake, Grandma struck up a conversation with the large and awkward man beside her. Somehow, the soft-spoken farmer had his way—but their descendents still remember the way they always fought. Those younger generations also recount the poignant end of the story, as Grandma lay dying three years after Grandpa had passed away. "Wait for me, my Beloved," she was said to whisper. "I'm coming now."

Grandma and Grandpa's coincidental meetings give the story an air of predestination. Clearly, they were fated to meet and marry—if they hadn't, the family that now exists would never have been born.

In other family stories, one woman wins out over many others for the love of a certain man. The attraction that families feel for this sort of story probably plays into the curiosity most children have at one time or another about "who would I be, if my father had married another woman?" The following story illustrates this concept.

When Great-Grandma Rose met her husband, she was already engaged to another man. The wedding was planned for the following summer, and her hope chest was stuffed and ready. Then the new pastor came to town. Grandma Rose took one look and instantly knew that this was the real thing. To the dismay of her family, she broke up with her fiancé and waited for the pastor to notice her. Eventually, he did . . . and the rest is family history.

Love stories add spice to family history.

Love stories like these give a family a sense that their own existence was foreordained, brought about by some divine plan or kindly fate. The stories add romance and meaning to ordinary life, and they serve to link siblings, aunts, uncles, and cousins together.

Family folklore comes in many forms—but whatever form it takes, it acts as a bond, one that unites not only present members of a family, but past and future ones as well.

Each family has its own unique identity.

THREE

How We
See Ourselves
Defining a Unique Identity

The relationship between mother and son helps to define these adults.

WHEN FAMILIES share the special stories and customs unique to their members, it fosters a sense of belonging among that specific group of people. "Folklore, being a familiar and creative way for people to relate to one another, also provides a social cohesiveness," says Simon J. Bronner in his book *American Children's Folklore*. Family folklore can both unite and divide.

At certain times of life, the children of a family use their own folklore to create a sense of cohesiveness among themselves, effectively excluding the family adults in their lives. "For children," Bronner says, ". . . want to declare their own identity, and lore is their protected expression of cultural connection to one another. . . ." Some siblings use secret languages to communicate, in a way that keeps outsiders from understanding them. For instance, two twin sisters recall that as children they shared a private "language," code words and secret meanings that only they could understand.

Special vocabularies also function to help define a unique family identity. In many families, a young child will have trouble with the standard pronunciation of a word or phrase, so she pronounces or says it in the best way she can. The family, charmed with this new version, may repeat it over and over, or even use it in place of the standard word or phrase.

Jan Harold Brunvand, in *The Study of American Folklore,* says: "Accounts of children's talk may qualify as folklore when they achieve oral circulation as part of a family's anecdotes. These are a few examples: "It's *winding*," "I *hood* it from you," and "We're *undusting*." Sometimes, a nonsense word can gain a unique signifi-

Families are treasure houses for stories, traditions, and love.

cance, as when a two-year-old, who was learning to talk and loved to combine odd words he had picked up, created the word "eggwater." The two-year-old is now a father himself, and for the members of his extended family, to be "full of eggwater," means to be full of silliness. Yet another young child could not pronounce her brother's name, Philip; no matter how hard she tried, it came out "Wutch"—and 40 years later, the family still speaks of Philip as Wutch.

In another family, the little girl routinely scrambled her syntax, so that "What does this mean?" always came out as "What means this?" The same child, frightened by tornadoes in lower Michigan, prayed fervently that Jesus would "take away the tomato storms, because you know I hate these tomato storms," much to the delight of the entire family. Both "What means this?" and "tomato storms" passed into the family's private lore.

Another little boy who was terrified of flies would chant, "Worried, worried, worried!" whenever an insect buzzed past him. In moments of tension or anxiety, 20 years later, his extended family is prone to lightening the moment by repeating, "Worried, worried, worried!"

Sometimes, euphemisms—usually for body functions considered unmentionable in polite conversations—are used among family members, creating a kind of secret code that only family understands. One family used the expression "Are we talking about camping?" as a code expression for such a body function. Just the use of this expression elicited smiles and gave each family member the feeling of being on the "inside" of a unit, a select society that excluded every other family in the world.

Sometimes lines from favorite books and movies are used in the same way. One family breaks up laughing each time a member says (to another member who has just done something less than brilliant), *You stoooooopid bunny!* This line comes from the movie *Watership Down*, and because of the context of the movie and the humor involved, no offense is taken by the use of the word "stupid."

Like many other mothers, an African American woman used family rituals and stories to give her daughters a strong sense of identity. Author Willi Coleman offers this memory:

Except for special occasions mama came home from work early on Saturdays. She spent six days a week mopping, waxing and dusting other women's houses. . . . Saturday nights were reserved for "taking care of them girls'" hair and the telling of stories. Some of which included a recitation of what she had endured and how she had triumphed over "folks that were lower than dirt" and "no-good snakes in the grass." She combed, patted, twisted, and talked. . . .

From Willi Coleman's "Closets and Keepsakes" in *Sage: A Scholarly Journal on Black Women* 4(2): 1987, pp. 34–35.

Children raised without the shelter of family folklore often suffer identity crises. For instance, the American government once shipped Native American children to boarding schools away from their families, hoping to erase their "Indian-ness," a terrible experience for these families. Parents complained that when their children returned home, they were strangers, no longer connected to them by the family's intimate and private bonds.

Other Native American children were sometimes placed in foster families. One woman who had suffered such a fate wrote:

Please help me find out who I am. My mother was Indian, but we were taken from her and put in foster homes. They wouldn't tell us anything, not even a story. . . . I don't remember now who I am.

Each member of a family has unique characteristics that are easily recognized by other members.

Folklore is not only passed from adults to children; children often shape a family's folklore as well.

Signals do not always need words. Some families use three quick squeezes of the hand to signal "I love you." Others use eye contact, winks, or other facial expressions.

Shared experiences are at the heart of defining a unique family identity. It is easy to understand the bonding effects of shared experiences when we observe veterans of World War II or the Vietnam War together; survivors of the Holocaust and other terrible tragedies immediately share common ground because of what they've been through together. In a less dramatic way (unless they've likewise shared tragedy), families form a bond through their common experiences.

"Remember when Billy fell out of the apple tree?"

"Remember how the cow crashed through the gate and got away?"

"Remember when Ida got stood up at the altar?"

"Remember when" acknowledges that the people in the conversation were there—together.

Some stories about forbears are told in order to highlight admirable behavior that adults hope their children will emulate. They hope to pass on the idea that their family is one with strong character qualities. This creates a family identity that helps the younger generation define who they are.

Even favorite cars may play a role in family stories.

One family, for instance, prides themselves on their kindness to animals. Each of the children knows that Great-Grandpa used to pick up the eight-legged creatures in his cupped hands and gently carry them outdoors. "Nice little fellow," he'd tell the spider. "You didn't want to hurt anybody, did you?"

Another family recalls the story of Great-Grandma's life in a war camp in North Africa during World War II. Grandma's strength and determination serves as examples to her descendents. After all, if she could survive (and clearly she did, or the family wouldn't be here today), current family members can also rise above whatever difficulties they face.

The story of Grandma's many lost children is also told in the same family. When a daughter-in-law suffered several miscarriages, the older generation of women comforted her with stories of the eight babies that Grandma lost, one right after another, before the mother-in-law and her younger brother finally survived long enough to grow into adulthood. Stories like these are offered as lessons in endurance and survival. They comfort and inspire—and they unite family members in a shared heritage. They tell the individual, "You are not alone."

Some stories aren't meant to teach anything—they're just

great stories that everyone enjoys. In *A Celebration of American Family Folklore,* William Hatch tells one he says has been told a "hundred thousand times in the family." When his Grandpa Hatch was a student at a Methodist College, he and some friends dumped over the dean's outhouse, while the dean was sitting inside. The college decided to expel them, but after much begging and pleading, the culprits were told they could stay if they bought and erected a new outhouse for the dean. They did so, and planned an on-campus dedication ceremony in front of a large crowd. They prayed and spoke and then sang the hymn "I Need Thee Every Hour"—and were promptly expelled from the college.

Another family recounts the time Aunt Ellie mysteriously disappeared when she was a little girl. The family thought she had drowned in the river or been kidnapped. Frantic with anxiety, they had no time to answer the call of nature. When one of them finally did make a quick trip to the family outhouse, they found the little girl jack-knifed in the hole, miserable and crying.

A single episode can represent the whole personality of a particular relative. Not many family members even remember Great Uncle Otto; in fact only one or two are still alive who met him personally but the whole family knows him because he is the one who worked in the bank the day it got robbed. He helped get the police by slipping out a side door; he was a hero. What else did Uncle Otto do during his lifetime? Nobody knows.

Sometimes, family folklore can be inaccurate and even destructive. Dad may be known as a jolly joker—when really his humor is cutting and destructive. Aunt Melissa may be the family's shy old maid—when really she is an intelligent and competent woman.

Traditional punishments also are a part of family folklore.

Sometimes, family characters are subject to caricature. "Who am I?" an eight-year-old asks his cousins, then sticks out his tummy and waddles. "Aunt Jenny! Aunt Jenny!" the cousins shout, talking about the aunt who is due to deliver her new baby within the week. The eight-year-old has picked out the most obvious feature about his Aunt Jenny to caricature. People do much the same thing with family members from the past.

"Remember how Ezelle always acted like a bull in a china shop?" a relative will ask, "stumbling through the room bumbling into first one piece of furniture and then another?" Family members often "emphasize a relative's most peculiar traits and habits in their folklore," say the authors of *A Celebration of American Family Folklore,* and they often give the relative a nickname that relates to the traits or habits. "Slugger" for the little ball

Fathers pass knowledge on to their sons.

Generations enjoy being togther.

player, "Sport" for the father who's anything but, "Tiny" for the biggest of the grown cousins; these nicknames identify not only a person but also his or her characteristics.

Some physical characteristics are hereditary, and become a source of folklore themselves—for instance, the Johnsons' long, thin nose; the Browns' stick-out ears; the Williamses' tiny feet. Personality characteristics become part of the folklore, also: the Perellis' sense of humor; the Clingmans' refusal to talk to each other before they've had their morning coffee. Less-than-savory qualities are prime material for family stories: Uncle Rhett who robbed the bank; Great Great Grandpa Dirk who was hanged as a horse thief. Because families observe each other's habits over the period of many years, they can sum up habits succinctly; one woman was known to lose her car keys so often that whenever she didn't show up for a family gathering on time, the family would roll their eyes and laugh, "She must have lost them again."

Even good qualities can be used in family folklore stories, usually by exaggerating stories about the good quality, and so making a "character" of the person described. One such story is about Aunt Arilla, who was the cleanest woman the Simpson family had ever met. She was known to wash her kitchen floor three times a day—and according to family tradition, she even scrubbed her driveway pavement on her hands and knees. And then there was Cousin Dick, who was known for his complete and utter honesty. Family members still chuckle over the time the church soprano asked him what he had thought of her solo. Uncle Dick shook his head sadly and said, "It sounded like the tom cat caterwauling outside my window last night."

Any unconventional behavior is grist for the family story mill, and stories sometime grow in the telling. One family loves to retell the story of Great Uncle Ned, who had a glass eye. When he was tired, he would pop the eye out of his socket and roll it around in his hand; once, he was said to have absent-mindedly set it down somewhere and forgotten about it—and, according to family legend, his son picked it up and lost it in a game of marbles, causing quite a family ruckus before the eye was returned to its proper place.

Family members are not only known by their behavior and physical characteristics; they often go down in family folklore for their quotes. The authors of *A Celebration of American Family Folklore* recount the story of a child who was visiting Washington, D.C., in an ice storm; she looked out the window and exclaimed, "Oh, mummy, it's so icy, horses are falling left and right!" When her mother questioned what she meant, the little girl admitted, "Well, one slipped." In that family now, "over-exaggeration in our family is always, 'Horses are falling left and right.' This is a seventy-year-old saying, but they all say it."

Families speak a kind of shorthand, made up of allusions to past experiences that do not have to be explained because members (who are on the "inside") all know the story. Implied in some such allusions are warnings or other messages. The Strodie family in the 1800s had a pig that was said to have "busted from too much buttermilk," and now, over a hundred years later, the saying "Remember Strodie's pig!" lives as a warning against overeating. When the boys of another family started out on a boat trip, one brother kissed his sister goodbye, then added "Tell Ma the boat floats." In that family, "Tell Ma the boat floats" is still used as an expression to tell other family members that everything is all right.

Marjorie Hunt, from McLean, Virginia, tells about a traveling peddler named Abediah. He visited her father's home in the Ozarks about twice a year and would always stay for dinner. Abediah talked excessively and interrupted frequently, so much so that years later, when family members interrupted each other, someone would invariably call out "Abediah!" and everyone knew instantly what was meant.

Every family has stories and traditions like these. If you think about it, you'll probably realize that your family has plenty of its own.

Families have always been places for sharing love.

FOUR

How We Relate
to Each Other
Sharing Love, Fighting Feuds

Families are small, close-knit "civilizations."

FROM THE EARLIEST pioneer days on, Americans have depended on each other for help and companionship. Communal work parties, such as barn-raisings, were essential to survival on the frontier, since no one person could "raise" a barn alone. Quilting bees, corn shuckings, house raisings, threshings, apple peelings—all these work parties were an outgrowth of the way Americans related to each other. Because extended families often lived in close proximity, these activities necessarily included many family members. Relatives, or "kin," were an essential part of growing up in a society that counted family as "social security." If a parent died, it was members of the extended family who stepped in and helped with chores and child raising. When parents or grandparents became unable to care for themselves, younger family members took them into their own homes or made sure they lived with another relative.

Today, though few citizens of the United States or Canada have ever participated in a barn raising, there are other customs by which people show support for one another. In our more mobile modern society, many members of the younger generation consider neighbors and friends a kind of family, and they function as one on some occasions. The "pound party" is one such occasion, when each person brings a pound of food or some other commodity to help a new neighbor or a new preacher set up housekeeping. Food showers are another such custom, as is the Harlem "rent party." Other customary family gatherings included spelling bees, square dances, ice-cream socials, box din-

The relationship between siblings is often one of both rivalry and intimacy.

ners, and hay rides; many of these activities now center around a church, another kind of "family."

These are gracious ways of relating to one another—with love and the intent to help. Traditions like the ones we've mentioned allow family members to reach past their own **insular** boundaries; helping hands pull outsiders into the shelter of a family's love and support.

But not all families behave this way. Families have an individual "style" to their relationships. One family laughs, plays games, and wrestles together; another family sits silently, absorbed in television shows for many hours a day. When one family quarrels at breakfast, they may go their separate ways in icy silence and never mention the issue again when they come back together for dinner. An old expression calls this "sweeping it under the rug," a reference to someone who sweeps a floor and is too lazy to dispose of the dirt properly, so lifts the rug and pushes the dirt underneath. Another family confronts disagreements squarely, sometimes venting emotions loudly, but always expressing love and forgiveness before moving on.

"There is a hard law . . . when an injury is done to us, we never recover until we forgive," says author Alan Paton. Families model either forgiveness or unforgiveness in the way they relate. Another author, Hannah Arendt, says, "Without being forgiven, released from the consequences of what we have done, our capacity to act would, as it were, be confined to a single deed from which we could never recover; we would remain the victims of its consequences forever, not unlike the sorcerer's apprentice who lacked the magic formula to break the spell."

Sometimes family members turn on each other, in conflicts small or large, brief or ongoing. Squabbles—little tiffs over not-so-important matters—make for good inter-family gossip. The authors of *A Celebration of American Family Folklore* tell of a man who went to his sister's house each morning to build a fire and do other household chores and was heard to sigh upon re-

Siblings need to work out daily conflicts.

turning to his own home. "I do my part," he said, "and speak to my sister on Monday, Wednesday, and Friday, but she won't do her part and speak to me on Tuesday and Thursday." Another family whispers about Aunt Mary and Uncle Del, who never had any children, apparently never shared a bed, and refuse to even share a house. Aunt Mary has the "big house," while Uncle Ned lives in the "little house," a cozy shed in the backyard. Their relatives wonder if Aunt Mary lets Ned come in to use the bathroom.

Serious conflict—adultery, divorce, lawbreaking—is usually hushed up when it's current, then turned into part of the family folklore much later. Things too painful to endure when they are happening often make good stories later on. In fact, sometimes the more shocking the behavior, the better the story. Even tragic tales of child abuse are repeated in one family—but the perpetrators are now long dead. In the words of one grandmother,

Authors Bossard and Boll, in *Ritual in Family Living,* describe the way certain small family rituals serve to connect family members over the years. (They define rituals as routine and customary behaviors, small traditions that remain the same from week to week and year to year.) These authors tell the story of an adult son who eats every Sunday dinner with his parents. After the meal, he always helps his mother with the dishes, while he tells her about the events of the week. His mother makes a pot of coffee while they work, and when they are done, they sit at the kitchen table and drink coffee, still talking. After a couple of hours, they rejoin the rest of the family (the man's father, wife, and children). The man always jokes that his mother had saved up dirty dishes from the entire week, and that was why it took him so long to help her.

Sharing a hobby knits family members together.

The mother-daughter relationship can be both tender and difficult.

My grandfather was a drinker. He worked hard for his family and supported them well, but he was not a nice man. He was cold and he had a temper, and when he had been drinking, he was pure evil. When my mother was a little girl, she was always glad when her father was away from home. More than once, after he'd been drinking, he threw her down the stairs in the night, from top to bottom. She had some bones in her ankle that never healed quite right.

Some conflicts among families are never resolved, and ongoing conflict can turn into a family feud. In an era when divorce, even multiple divorce, is so prevalent, there are plenty of "sides" to go to war. Other relationships split over money, including inheritances and family-owned businesses or land. Sometimes the feud is between family members; at other times, family members step in to defend or revenge one of "their own," and another family or families are embroiled in the fight. This is what happened in Shakespeare's famous play, *Romeo and Juliet*. Many times, however, the fight is kept within the family and enters the collection of family folklore.

"Oh, Grandma doesn't talk to Aunt Lucy," one friend told me.

"They haven't spoken ever since their mother died 20 years ago. My grandmother wanted her mother's embroidered pillowcases and tablecloths, but her sister got them. According to Grandma, she just walked right in the house, while poor Grandma was still at the viewing, and took them, without even asking anyone. The first Grandma knew what happened was when she saw one of the tablecloths on Aunt Lucy's table the next Thanksgiving. Grandma's never forgiven her. She probably never will. I think they both like it this way, actually. It gets them more attention, you know, with all of us having to run around and communicate for them at family gatherings."

Family relationships can be loving and difficult at the same time.

The relationship between siblings can be a tense one, fraught
with jealousy and rivalry—at any
age, apparently. Mothers and
daughters also have complicated
relationships, and many folklore
stories deal with it. The following
story was brought to North America by Lebanese immigrants.

A widow had an only child, a
lovely daughter, who became seri-
ously ill. The illness went on a long
time, and all the girl could do was
lie on a bed near a window and gaze out at the one tree in the
yard.

When autumn came, the leaves fell from the tree one by one,
and the daughter became convinced that when the last leaf fell,
she too would die. She shared this belief with her mother, whose
heart ached at the thought of losing her precious girl.

One cold, windy night the mother saw that only one leaf re-
mained on the tree. After her daughter fell asleep, she went outside into the stormy, freezing weather to the wall behind the tree
and painted a picture of the last leaf, a picture so perfect that it
looked exactly like the real leaf, which had now fallen.

In the morning the daughter saw that one leaf still clung to
the tree. After many days, and then many weeks, the leaf was still
there. The girl took courage from the sight of the leaf and began
to recover. The mother, however, became very ill from going out
into the stormy night. Her illness became tuberculosis and she
died. When the daughter was at last fully recovered, she was able
to go outside to see how the one remaining leaf still clung to the
tree, and there she discovered what her mother had done for her.

Then she realized how much her mother loved her, and how much she had sacrificed for her.

No matter how difficult, the relationships between family members are in most cases strong and life giving. From our families, these tiny, intimate "civilizations," we learn how to relate to the rest of the world. We gain the interpersonal skills we need for our professional lives—as well as the skills we will need to one day create families of our own.

Parents shape our concept of God, forming a family faith heritage.

FIVE

How We See God
Glimpsing the Divine

A Jewish father passes his faith on to his son.

Because parents are the first adults and the first authority figures that children ever know, parents' characters shape their children's idea of God forever, for good or ill. In the Christian New Testament, Jesus tells a story about an ideal father, the kind of father that everyone would like to have. This father was forgiving and loving and generous. The story of the prodigal son is meant to show what kind of father God is.

When parents and other adults are cruel or uncaring, their behaviors also shape the way children see God. Roberta Bondi, a church history professor, had a harsh and distant father when she was growing up. He was intolerant of any weakness, imperfection, or disobedience. Questioning and asking why was not permitted.

Roberta's father left her family before she was 12 years old. After that, she saw him only once a year. Although she was a religious person, for many years, whenever she heard someone refer to God as "the Father," she struggled with anger and distaste, a sense of revulsion that took her years to overcome. For her family, the word "father" had come to have a private meaning, one that was almost synonymous with "ogre" or "villain." No wonder then that Roberta cringed when she heard this word applied to God.

Luckily, not all family folklore leaves such a bad taste in the mouth. Much of it is positive and creative. Although adults may leave the faith of their parents, they will nevertheless retain an entire body of tradition and lore that cannot be erased. For instance, one man, a professed agnostic, still thinks of rainstorms

Informal conversations with parents often do as much to shape our ideas about life and God as do more formal religious training.

as "God's tears," because that was what his mother always said when he was a child. He also confesses that whenever he's scared, he finds himself muttering a prayer his mother invented:

Dear God, such fright!
Don't let Satan bite.
Keep me safe, I pray,
To live another day.

No matter what we believe intellectually, family folklore sticks in the mind.

Families also teach their children about God in a more formal way, through the rituals and traditions of their church, or by seeing that their children go through organized training, such as learning their **catechism.** But much of what a child picks up about God is learned from small family rituals, like before-meal grace and bedtime prayer.

Sometimes, a family member may rebel against a family tradition and refuse to pass it on to the next generation. For instance, one woman grew up saying this familiar prayer:

Now I lay me down to sleep,
I pray the Lord my soul to keep.

If I should die before I wake,
I pray the Lord my soul to take.

When this woman was a child, bedtime was filled with dread and uneasiness. The words of the prayer acted as a constant reminder that one day she would die; she worried that she might, in fact, die that very night, and she would lie awake with her heart pounding, afraid to fall asleep for fear that she might "die before she woke." So when she became an adult, she instituted a very different family tradition.

She wanted her children to connect God with joy and gratitude rather than fear, so each night they did "glads":

"I'm glad, God, that the sun was shining today."
"I'm glad, God, that Susie could come over and play."
"I'm glad, God, that Tammy isn't sick anymore."
"I'm glad, God, that you made our kitten."

Passing on the family faith is considered a sacred responsibility in many Jewish families. In the fifth book of the Old Testament, God told the Jews:

Christ warned us by his life and death, so who am I that I should not warn my daughter by my life?

—*Yula Moses, quoted by Daryl Cumber Dance*

Hear, O Israel: The Lord our God, the Lord is one. Love the Lord your God with all your heart and with all your soul and with all your strength. These commandments that I give you today are to be upon your hearts. Impress them on your children. Talk about them when you sit at home and when you walk along the road, when you lie down and when you get up. Tie them as symbols on your hands and bind them on your foreheads. Write them on the doorframes of your houses and on your gates. (Deuteronomy 6: 4–9)

(This is part of the Shema, the Jewish confession of faith.)

The Jewish people have devised many traditions and symbols to help pass along their heritage to their children. The bar mitzvah and bas (or bat) mitzvah are two of the most important ceremonies. Symbols, which often come to be considered heirlooms, are also important in passing on customs and traditions. For many Jewish families, the family menorah is an important symbol of Hanukkah; the prayer shawl used by a father or grandfather is also important. In a touching story by Sheldon Oberman,

Passing on the family faith is a sacred responsibility for many Jewish families.

THE PRODIGAL SON

There was a man who had two sons. The younger one said to his father, "Father, give me my share of the estate." So he divided his property between them. Not long after that, the younger son got together all he had, set off for a distant country and there squandered his wealth in wild living. After he had spent everything, there was a severe famine in that whole country, and he began to be in need. So he went and hired himself out to a citizen of that country, who sent him to his fields to feed pigs. He longed to fill his stomach with the pods that the pigs were eating, but no one gave him anything.

When he came to his senses, he said, 'How many of my father's hired men have food to spare, and here I am starving to death! I will set out and go back to my father and say to him: Father, I have sinned against heaven and against you. I am no longer worthy to be called your son; make me like one of your hired men." So he got up and went to his father.

But while he was a still a long way off, his father saw him and was filled with compassion for him; he ran to his son, threw his arms around him and kissed him.

The son said to him, "Father, I have sinned against heaven and against you. I am no longer worthy to be called your son."

But the father said to his servants, "Quick! Bring the best robe and put it on him. Put a ring on his finger and sandals on his feet. Bring the fattened calf and kill it. Let's have a feast and celebrate. For this son of mine was dead and is alive again; he was lost and is found." So they began to celebrate. . . . (Luke 15:8–24, New International Version)

Our view of both the physical and spiritual worlds is shaped by what our parents taught us when we were very young.

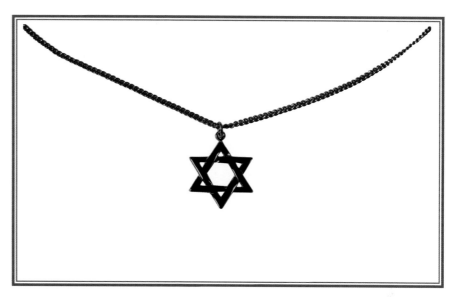

A piece of jewelry can symbolize a family's heritage of faith.

called *The Always Prayer Shawl*, a grandfather's cherished prayer shawl, used first in Europe and later brought to America, is at last passed on to his grandson, creating a tangible link between generations of Jewish men who loved and honored their God.

Christian families also sometimes pass on religious symbols, such as the family Bible, to the younger generation. One Catholic grandmother gave her granddaughter her silver rosary, teaching her the Italian words to the prayer that she herself had been taught as a child. The rosary had once belonged to the grandmother's grandmother, and it created a link of both faith and sentiment between the generations.

Religious folklore may be shared by an entire community, but because the experience of the divine is often a private matter, many faith traditions are also private, shared only with those to whom one is closest—the family. One mother and daughter may

The "Holy Family" is a model for some Christian families.

say *compline* together every night by candlelight; another family has a simple grace they say before each meal:

Dear Jesus, bless our food and bless our day,
Bless our work and bless our play.
Amen.

Yet another family goes around the table at every Thanksgiving dinner, saying the things for which they are particularly thankful to God. Adult children may continue to tell the story of the "miracle" that saved their father from certain death when he was sick with lung cancer, teaching the younger generation that the divine is a real and loving force in the family's life.

All of these are forms of family folklore that shape the concept of God. Each of these small, private traditions offers yet another glimpse at something that is invisible. Family folklore often makes tangible that which can't be touched, and it allows family members to see with the eyes of faith.

Birthday celebrations are important events in family folklore.

SIX

Handling Change and
the Passage of Time
Celebration and Mourning

Family outings can become celebrations that mark the passage of time.

To CHILDREN, physical growth is a kind of marker that shows their dream is coming true—they are growing into adults. Every quarter inch marked on the wall or growth chart, every baby tooth lost, every birthday, signals that they are one step closer to their goal. Traditions have grown up around these markers, and loving families make children feel secure by the observance of customs associated with the passage of time.

LOST TEETH

When children lose baby teeth, it is a common custom to have the child place the tooth beneath his pillow. The "tooth fairy" is said to come during the night and exchange the child's tooth for money. When the child wakes up, he finds the money and gets to keep it.

Various family traditions have evolved around this North American custom. Some family's have the tooth fairy write little notes to the child. Other families have a special silver cup where the tooth is placed (easier for the fairy to find, since pillows must be hard to lift for such a tiny creature). Some parents allow their children to know that it is all "pretend," while others insist to children that the tooth fairy is real. Many parents long to have their children maintain their faith in the imaginary world of tooth fairies and Santa Claus for as long as possible. Perhaps this fantasy world is something grownups wish they could recapture, and so they get to experience it **vicariously** through their children. In any case, the family traditions surrounding lost teeth are often satisfying and fun for both children and adults.

BIRTHDAYS

Many families have their own unique birthday customs, but some customs are common to a large majority of American families.

On the day when the child is first born, the attention is focused mainly on that small new person. From the beginning of their lives, children are traditionally dressed in colors that indicate their sex—pink for girls, blue for boys. In many families, the fathers hand out some small gift in celebration of the new family member. Cigars were the gift of choice before the dangers of tobacco smoking were widely known and accepted; some fathers now choose Tootsie Rolls or candy cigars. Naming ceremonies, christenings, infant baptisms (including the choosing of **godparents**), and dedications, all continue the focus on the new person in the family.

The birthday as an annual celebration of the original birth day once again focuses attention on the person. Some families make the entire day special by making sure the birthday person

Each family has its own birthday traditions.

The dreidel, a wooden top, is one of the symbols used to celebrate Hanukkah, but no one seems exactly sure of why this is so. Throughout Jewish history, some rulers have forbidden Jews to study the Torah, or to practice their religion. It is thought that sometimes, when Jews were studying the Torah, they may have kept a dreidel at hand so that if soldiers appeared they could pretend to be playing with one of the tops. The dreidel could also have come from the spinning top the Germans had as far back as medieval times. Symbols are put on the sides of the dreidel, and a game is played that depends on the symbol that comes up when the top is spun.

does no normal chores or other work. Other families allow the birthday person to chose an activity, such as a visit to a zoo or an amusement park, for the special day.

Special attention is often shown by serving carefully prepared food. A common custom is allowing the person to chose her favorite food for the birthday meal; this is followed by serving a birthday cake with candles (most often one candle for each year, plus one for "good luck"), and ice cream. The birthday person takes a deep breath, silently makes a wish, then blows the candles out. If she manages to blow out all the candles at once, her wish will come true.

The birthday meal is usually followed by giving wrapped presents to the birthday person. Some parents write yearly letters to their children, commenting on the growth they've seen in them in the previous year, and assuring them of their never-ending love. Other family celebrations are more raucous and include pretend "spankings," with the birthday person receiving a number of "spanks" equal to his age, plus "one to grow on." "Pinch day," "hit day," and "kiss day" sometimes precede or follow the actual birthday in some regions of the country.

Here are two other birthday customs, from Simon J. Bronner's *American Children's Folklore:*

- Your friends catch the birthday person and either punch them on the arm, giving them their birthday whacks, or pull their earlobes according to how old they are plus one for good luck.
- As each present is brought out to be opened, it is held over the birthday person's head (so he can't see who it is from). This rhyme is repeated, and the birthday person makes a wish for the giver for the next year (e.g., "May you get your heart's desire," "May you have a hot romance," etc.):

Heavy, heavy hangs over thy head
What do you wish for this person, with a bump on the head?
(Bang present on person's head.)

The most special birthdays are those that mark certain milestone ages. When a Jewish boy turns 13 (the age of religious duty and responsibility), a bar mitzvah is held to mark his coming of age. For a Jewish girl in non-Orthodox congregations, the counterpart is a bas mitzvah (or bat mitzvah), which also marks her

A birthday party is a favorite custom.

Graduation is a "coming of age" celebration.

attaining religious adulthood. Girls in America used to celebrate their "Sweet Sixteen" birthday; girls in Mexican families often have a special celebration for their 15th birthday, called *quinciñeros*.

Coming of age for both boys and girls can mean gaining new privileges (and the age for different privileges differs with each family). In earlier times, boys marked their new maturity by wearing long pants, while girls let the hems of their dresses down or put their hair up. Today's families have their own private ways to recognize family members' coming of age in small, informal ways. In more wealthy families, a child may get a car of his own on his 16th birthday. A girl may be allowed to get her ears pierced in honor of her 13th birthday. Your mother probably still remembers the first time she was allowed to wear nylons or high heels and the first time she shaved her legs; your father may recall shaving his face for the first time. For you, it may be having the freedom to date when you turn a certain age, or being given a later curfew.

CELEBRATING THE SEASONS AND TIMES

Bedtime is often associated with family rituals or customs. Many families have bedtime prayers; many read aloud. Sometimes one

Hanukkah comes in either late November or in December. If you use the Hebrew calendar, which is based on the moon's movement around the sun and has only 354 days instead of 365, Hanukkah begins at sundown on the 25th day of Kislev (the ninth month). Hanukkah, which means "rededication," is also known as the festival of lights, and is held in celebration of a miracle that occurred over 2,000 years ago.

When King Antiochus brought his large Syrian army to Jerusalem to force the Jews to worship Greek gods, he ruined the Jews' Temple and tried to destroy their religion. By the time Judah Maccabee (the name means "hammer" and was given to Judah because of the way he struck blows against Antiochus) and his brothers won back Jerusalem from the Syrians, the Temple was in disrepair. There was a special menorah in the Temple—a seven-branched oil lamp that was always supposed to remain lit—and the Maccabees relit it. Although there was only enough oil to burn for one day, the menorah stayed lit for eight days, which gave the Jews time enough to make a new supply of oil. On the 25th day of Kislev, in 165 BCE, the Temple was made holy again, or "rededicated," and Judah Maccabee declared the day a holiday.

favorite book is read over and over at the child's request, perhaps for months. Several families report reading Margaret Wise Brown's *Good Night, Moon* in this way.

Sometimes parents teach children to greet the approaching darkness, marked by the appearance of the first star, by saying this poem:

Star light, star bright,
First star I see tonight,
I wish I may, I wish I might,
Have this wish I wish tonight.

The child then makes a secret wish (and perhaps the parents do, too).

The change of seasons is sometimes marked by activities tied to national holidays. Often, Labor Day weekend is used as an end-of-the-summer get away, in some families combined with putting away the boat and bringing in the dock for the winter, or shrouding the cabin furniture with dust sheets, thus marking an official end of the summer season and the beginning of the autumn.

Some change-of-season customs are unique to individual families. One family celebrates spring by going on a picnic the day that any family member first sights a robin—rain or shine, freezing weather or balmy.

While playing pranks on April Fool's Day may be a national custom, folklore in general becomes the folklore of a specific family by the specific pranks that are played (the more successful of these pranks are often told and retold with glee through the years). Mother's Day, Father's Day, and Grandparents' Day are also national customs, but each family's observance differs widely. For example, one family celebrates Mother's Day the same way each year: the children (who are now teenagers) prepare their mother a bowl of Frosted Flakes with strawberries on it and bring it to her while she is still in bed. Another family always goes for a

Family vacations celebrate the seasons.

Celebrating life-cycle events and holidays often sets the stage for family storytelling. . . . Tales are not told simply to jar our memories. A bride and bridegroom do not forget the tricks a cousin pulled at their wedding. A mother hardly needs to be reminded where her children were when she gave birth to the youngest. . . . Such tales are, rather, the sound of a family very much in the present, celebrating, renewing, and reestablishing itself through its stories.

—Steven J. Zeitlin, Amy J. Kotkin, Holly Cutting Baker,
    A Celebration of Family Folklore

hike on Mother's Day (the mother's favorite activity, which other family members do not enjoy as much as she); and yet another family shoots off model rockets every Father's Day.

Thanksgiving is considered by many to be one of the most important American holidays, a combination of a harvest festival and a day for giving thanks to God for his blessings. Most Thanksgiving customs center around the traditional dinner, and many families use that time to give thanks in creative ways. One example is the custom of putting grains of corn at each place setting. The corn represents the food given to the Pilgrims by the Native Americans—food which saved the Pilgrims' lives—and 21st-century Americans who follow this tradition share with the others around the table as many things for which they are thankful as they have grains of corn by their plates.

CHRISTMAS

So many customs and traditions are associated with Christmas that perhaps every family has at least one that is unique. This is the way author Bebe Faas Rice remembers Christmas in her house in Iowa in the 1940s: They opened all their presents on Christmas Eve, with what Rice calls "No Christmas morning see-what-Santa-brought bonanza for us." Christmas Day was a time for going to church and for having relatives over for the annual Christmas dinner.

The Christmas Eve dinner would feature their father's oyster stew and their mother's homemade bread (because Roman Catholics of that time ate no meat on Christmas Eve), and dinner was eaten in the living room by the light of candles. Rice and her sister would light a lantern in the window to "guide the Christ child through the dark streets," while her father helped ready the turkey and her mother prepared corn bread stuffing for the next

Christmas traditions are an important aspect of family folklore.

Today's family traditions may be shaped by long-ago family members.

day's dinner. They opened gifts at nine o'clock, with only the tree lights lit to illumine the unwrapping of gifts.

Some families have very unique traditions. For instance, one family has the annual "burying Aunt Lillian." After all the presents are opened, the children in the family gather up the ripped wrapping paper in great crackling armfuls. Down on the floor goes 70-year-old Aunt Lillian. And then paper flies with wild abandon and shrieks of excitement, until not a bit of Aunt Lillian's staid navy blue dress can be seen. The children fall silent, half horrified by this strange and exciting moment. Then the paper shifts, just slightly, and one pale, bony finger extends upward. This is the signal for more shrieks, more wildly tossed paper, until again Aunt Lillian is obliterated from view. Several similar rounds ensue—until the adults take pity on Aunt Lillian and gather up the wrapping paper in garbage bags. The children, trying to calm themselves from all the excitement, are already looking forward to next year.

HANUKKAH AND PASSOVER

For Jewish families, Hanukkah is a significant holiday that includes songs, games, plays, and special foods. When people celebrate Hanukkah today, they use certain symbols and customs to remind them of the story behind this special eight-day holiday. The menorah, an eight-branched candelabrum, reminds those who see it of the menorah in the Temple so many years ago. Although it has eight branches, it actually holds nine candles. The taller candle in the center is called the *shammash*, which means "servant" or "helper," and is used to light the other eight candles, a new one for each night of the holiday until all are lit. When the shammash is lit, these prayers are said over it before it is used to light the other candles:

> *Blessed art thou, O Lord our God, ruler of the universe, who has sanctified us with his commandments and commanded us to kindle the Hanukkah lights.*

> *Blessed art thou, O Lord our God, ruler of the universe, who performed miracles for our forefathers in those days, at this time.*

A bar mitzvah is an occasion for family and faith.

Families who celebrate the passage of time also have opportunities for getting together and enjoying each other.

The following prayer is made on the first night of Hanukkah:

Blessed art thou, O Lord our God, ruler of the universe, who has granted us life, sustained us, and enabled us to reach this occasion.

Jewish families seldom make as big a deal out of Hanukkah as most Christian families do over Christmas; gift-giving tends to be more modest. One woman recalls that her grandparents always gave her a shiny silver coin for each day of Hanukkah; a man remembers one special Hanukkah when he received a volume of the Hardy Boys for each day of the holiday.

Another Jewish holiday, Passover, shows how traditions change when transplanted to another country, in this case, America. The traditional "search for leaven" was originally conducted with a candle and a quill. Now it is done with a flashlight and a brush. A ritual cleansing of dishes and utensils was performed in preparation for the Passover, but now many Jewish families have a special set of dishes just for holiday use. **Matzoh**, which once required careful handwork, can now be made easily using a matzoh machine. In spite of these changes, however, the holiday itself is still a cherished tradition in many American Jewish families. Each family adds its own flavor, its own unique stories, games, and songs that have become connected with the season. One family always invites guests to share Passover with them. Another woman complains about the gefilte fish that her family eats for the holiday. "My grandmother always made it," she remembers, "and we all hated it and made jokes about it when she wasn't around. But now that she's dead, my mother makes the gefilte fish, just the way Grandma did. Someday, I'll probably be making it too."

Courtship has its own traditions.

COURTSHIP AND MARRIAGE

As one of the most joyous of occasions, courtship and marriage have some of the most interesting customs. Romantic relationships were long the exclusive territory of the family. Parents were never far out of earshot when a young man came calling. Young people were seldom left unsupervised. (Bundling, a courting custom that seemed to flaunt the other conventions and allowed unmarried couples to occupy the same bed without undressing, was the most obvious exception to this rule.) Today, however, confining one's time with a sweetheart to the family parlor or the porch swing has long gone out of style, giving way to "dating." The advent of the car made young people far more mobile and gave them greater privacy. But engaged couples still routinely show their exclusive attachment by buying a diamond ring, and showers are still given for the bride-to-be, to ensure the couple has all the basic necessities to set up housekeeping. The groom-to-be is still likely to be feted with a "stag party."

Many customs are associated with the wedding itself. How the attendants are chosen, how the guests are seated, the custom of kissing the bride, banging spoons against glassware at the reception to induce the couple to kiss publicly, throwing rice (and now birdseed in deference to the wildlife), or blowing bubbles when the newly married woman appears—these are all done in accordance with long-established custom.

Less genteel is the custom of harassing the bridal couple, preferably with a great deal of noise. This custom, known as a shivaree, has its roots in the Old World custom of *charivari*. Precursors to the shivaree (often perpetrated by family members and recited for years to come) can include tricks played at the wedding. There are many reports of family members writing funny sayings ("Help me!") on the soles of the groom's shoes, so that when he kneels at the altar with his new bride, the audience is left laughing. In another family, a note was left inside the cap of the gas tank so that attendants read "Help, I'm being kidnapped!" Tin cans or other noisemakers are often tied to the car in which the couple plans to leave the wedding; the car is traditionally "decorated," with signs or drawings, so that everyone the couple passes knows instantly that this is a newly married couple. The shivaree itself involves waking the newly married couple with raucous noise and forcing them outside to greet or treat the peo-

Weddings are occasions for tradition.

Bride and mother are linked by generations of family folklore.

ple involved. In one family, family members have been known to welcome the newly married couple back to their new home by removing the labels from all their canned goods.

Because people of many nationalities have made America their home, the customs of families from other lands are becoming more prevalent. For instance, there are now many Pakistani immigrants in North America. It is a tradition in some Pakistani families that the flower girl has her hands painted in a certain orange-red design called *mehndi* in preparation for the wedding. The intricate design covers both of her hands with flowers and stars and swirling patterns.

MOURNING

Death customs are connected to our innate fears and superstitions. One old custom associated with death is to pour all water out of the vases in the house; another is to stop the clocks throughout the house. Some families once draped the furniture in the room where a corpse lies, as a mark of respect. Others left the tools used for digging lying by the grave for several days.

Today's families have their own mourning traditions. In some families a will is used to divide up the possessions of the person who has died to other family members; in others, family members simply agree on who wants what, often with the eldest child choosing first. Families often put poems or death notices in the classified section of the local newspaper, and in some regions special days to work in the cemetery are observed. Memorial Day is one in which people often place flowers at a loved one's grave.

Ways of remembering the departed loved one are often unique to each family. For instance, one family keeps the jar of

Faith offers families hope in the face of death.

change Dad once used for family poker games; each New Year's Eve, the adult brothers and sisters play poker to determine who gets to be the keeper of the jar for the following year. In yet another family, the mother cooks with her mother's set of pots and pans every year on her mother's birthday.

FAMILY traditions like these are important for marking the passage of time. Whether time brings us new joys—as with the birth of a child or an adolescent's coming of age—or whether time robs us of loved ones, family celebrations help us structure life's big events. By celebrating together our joy is increased; mourning as a family, our sadness is lessened.

A family is a chain of tradition and love that reaches into the future.

SEVEN

A Heritage for the Future

The Family's Never-Ending Chain

Long-ago ancestors left a heritage of family folklore.

FAMILIES HAVE been the building block of successful civilizations since the beginning of history. It is within the secure and loving confines of a family that children learn, as Edith Schaeffer says, to be affected, inspired and helped by other family members. They can draw strength from the deep roots the family has in the past; they can find hope as they envision the family stretching out into the future.

When children are grounded in the customs and traditions of their forebears, they find the stability that comes from belonging, and the sense of self-worth that comes from being accepted unconditionally. Then these children, in turn, can pass along the same stability and unconditional acceptance to the generations to come. Family folklore is one of the most important vehicles for transmitting family history, customs, traditions—and love.

The folklore of your own family is a reality, whether you're aware of it or not, but you might want to begin a collection of family stories, traditions, and words, things that are unique to your family. In a way, this isn't so very different from keeping a family picture album or creating home movies; it's a way of recording family life so that future generations can enjoy it.

Try interviewing older members of your family, so that you can capture their unique perspectives. They may have family stories you've never heard before. The authors of *A Celebration of Family Folklore* offer some suggestions for recording family stories. The suggestions that follow are adapted from their list:

The authors of *A Celebration of Family Folklore* give some suggestions for creating an informal questionnaire to use as a starting point for collecting family folklore. Here are some of the questions they suggest using:

1. What do you know about your family surname? Did it change at all when the family immigrated to North America? Are there any stories about that change?
2. Are there any traditional naming practices in your family? Are there any common first names that have been used generation after generation?
3. Are there any **notorious** figures in the family's past?
4. How did your parents and grandparents meet and fall in love?
5. What are the favorite recipes in your family?
6. What are your family's most important heirlooms?
7. Are there any unique expressions or words used in your family?

1. Start with a question or topic you know will lead to a full answer, such as a story you've heard that family member tell before. This will give your relative confidence.
2. Avoid asking questions that are too general. For instance, don't start out with, "Tell me about your childhood?" Think about it; what would *you* say if someone asked you something so vague? Instead, try to think of something particular to ask, like "How old were you when you got your first car?" and then go from there.
3. Avoid asking yes-or-no questions. These seldom will lead to an interesting story.
4. Respect your relative's privacy. There may be some topics he or she is not comfortable discussing.

Families are a storehouse for fascinating stories.

5. Show interest. Interject comments wherever it's appropriate. Look at your relative while he or she talks.
6. Don't worry if your relative goes off on a tangent without ever answering your question. You may hear another story that's just as interesting.
7. Use props; old letters, scrapbooks, photograph albums, home movies, or family heirlooms can help get a conversation going.
8. Be sensitive to your relative's reactions. If they're elderly, be aware that they may tire easily. Be ready to quit when they are.

The relationship between your grandmother and her mother may even influence the relationship between you and your mother.

Family game times are a part of family folklore.

9. Be aware that other family members may feel jealous of the attention you're paying to a particular person. Try to give everyone a chance to participate in your "family folklore collecting."

10. If possible, prepare some sort of tangible collection of the stories and material you gather. Make a scrapbook, create a written account, or make a home movie. That way the entire family can feel the satisfaction of your project—and you can hand it on to the next generation, creating a heritage for the future.

Further Reading

Battle, Kemp P., compiler. *Great American Folklore: Legends, Tales, Ballads and Superstitions from All Across America.* Garden City: Doubleday, 1986.

Bronner, Simon J. American *Children's Folklore: A Book of Rhymes, Games, Jokes, Stories, Secret Languages, Beliefs and Camp Legends.* Little Rock, Ark.: August Books, 1988.

Gardella, Tricia, compiler. *Writers In the Kitchen.* Honesdale: Boyds Mills Press, 1998.

Yolen, Jane and Stemple, Heidi E. Y. *Mirror, Mirror: Forty Folktales for Mothers and Daughters to Share.* New York: Penguin Putnam, 2000.

Zeitlin, Steven J., Kotkin, Amy J., and Baker, Holly Cutting. *A Celebration of American Family Folklore.* Cambridge: Yellow Moon Press, 1982.

For More Information

Aaron Shepard's Home Page
www.aaronshep.com/stories/

American Folklore
americanfolklore.net/folktales/

American Folklore Society
afsnet.org

Children's Folklore
ausis.gf.vu.lt/eka/childfolk/teasing.html

Folk and Fairy Tales
www.pitt.edu/~dash/folklinks.html

Story Lore
tech-head.com/story.htm

Glossary

Archives Records, historical documents.

Baby boomers The generation born during the period of increased births after World War II.

Catechism A summary of religious doctrine often in the form of questions and answers.

Compline The last "hour" before bedtime, observed by some religious people as a time for prayer.

Daguerreotypes Early photographs produced on a silver or a silver-covered copper plate.

Depression The period of decreased economic activity from about 1929 to 1939.

Ethnography The descriptive study of traditions in a specific group or region.

Folklife The full traditional lore, behavior, and material culture of a group of people.

Godparents Sponsors at a baptism who agree to help the child, spiritually and physically, throughout his or her life.

Insular Separated from others.

Matzoh Unleavened bread; used especially at Passover

Mobile Movable.

Nostalgia A sense of yearning for the past.

Notorious Well-known, usually for a negative reason.

Superseded To take the place, room, or position; to force out of use as inferior.

Vicariously Experienced through imagined identification with another person

Index

Biographies

Shirley Brinkerhoff is a writer, editor, speaker, and musician. She graduated from Cornerstone University with a Bachelor of Music degree, and from Western Michigan University with a Master of Music degree. She has published six young adult novels, three nonfiction books for young adults, scores of short stories and articles, and teaches at writers' conferences throughout the United States.

Ellyn Sanna is the author of more than 50 books. She is also the mother of three children, who are creating their own collection of family folklore.

Dr. Alan Jabbour is a folklorist who served as the founding director of the American Folklife Center at the Library of Congress from 1976 to 1999. Previously, he began the grant-giving program in folk arts at the National Endowment for the Arts (1974–1876). A native of Jacksonville, Florida, he was trained at the University of Miami (B.A.) and Duke University (M.A., Ph.D.). A violinist from childhood on, he documented old-time fiddling in the Upper South in the 1960s and 1970s. A specialist in instrumental folk music, he is known as a fiddler himself, an art he acquired directly from elderly fiddlers in North Carolina, Virginia, and West Virginia. He has taught folklore and folk music at UCLA and the University of Maryland and has published widely in the field.